The Great Roadrunner Race

adapted by Sarah Willson

based on a screenplay written by Leyani Diaz

illustrated by Alex Maher

Ready-to-Read

Simon Spotlight/Nickelodeon
New York   London   Toronto   Sydney

Based on the TV series *Go, Diego, Go!*™ as seen on Nick Jr.®

SIMON SPOTLIGHT
An imprint of Simon & Schuster Children's Publishing Division
1230 Avenue of the Americas, New York, New York 10020
Library of Congress Cataloging-in-Publication Data
Willson, Sarah.
The great roadrunner race / by Sarah Willson ; illustrated by Alex Maher. —
1st ed.
p. cm. — (Ready-to-read)
"Based on the TV series Go, Diego, Go! as seen on Nick Jr."
At head of title: Nick Jr. /Diego.
ISBN: 978-1-4169-7867-1
I. Maher, Alex, ill. II. Go, Diego, go! (Television program) III. Title.
PZ7.W6845Gre 2009
[E] — dc22
2008026691

Hi! I am !
DIEGO

This is my friend .
ROADY

He has a big today.
RACE

The is for .
RACE   ROADRUNNERS

 are birds.

ROADRUNNERS

They do not fly.

But  are good

ROADRUNNERS

runners.

In this  RACE ROADY needs to
run and duck.

He needs to
jump and shake.

We can help him practice!

Beep! Beep!

It is my sister  .

ALICIA

She says we have to hurry!

The 🏁 will begin soon.

RACE

We need to practice!

I will drink some .
WATER

 will eat a .
ROADY   PEAR

He gets from the .
JUICE   PEAR

and I run up a **.**

ROADY   HILL

Then we run down.

Be careful, !

ROADY

Watch out for the  !

CACTUS

Next, we practice ducking.

Duck, !

ROADY

Duck under that !

CACTUS

Show  how to duck.

ROADY

You duck too!

Now we practice jumping.

Jump, !

ROADY

Jump over the 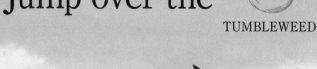!

TUMBLEWEED

Show  how to jump.
ROADY

You jump too!

Uh-oh! A  storm!
SAND

What can protect us from the  storm?

SAND

We need help from !

RESCUE PACK

Yes! A 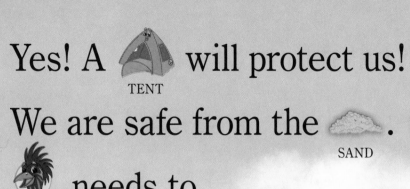 will protect us!
TENT

We are safe from the ☁.
SAND

🐦 needs to
ROADY

shake away the ☁.
SAND

Shake, shake, shake!

Will you show how to shake?

ROADY

You shake too!

Shake, shake, shake!

We did it!

Good shaking!

And here we are

at the  RACE.

The racers must do **3**
things:

duck under the  ,
PARACHUTE

jump over the , and
HURDLES

shake away the .
SAND

Ready . . . set . . . go!
Run, , run!

ROADY

There is the  !

PARACHUTE

Duck, !

ROADY

He ducked!

Here are the  HURDLES!

Jump, ROADY!

He jumped!

Next comes the  !
SAND

Shake, ROADY , shake!

He shook!

The 🏁 is over!

RACE

 won!

ROADY

Hooray for !

ROADY

Thanks for helping!